Angela Anaconda™

FLOUR POWER

POCKET BOOKS

Based on the TV series *Angela Anaconda*®
created by Joanna Ferrone and Sue Rose as seen on Channel 4

First published in 2001 by Pocket Books
An imprint of Simon & Schuster UK Limited
Africa House, 64-78 Kingsway, London WC2B 6AH

ISBN 07434 28854

1 3 5 7 9 10 8 6 4 2

Printed in Hong Kong by Midas

CONTENTS

Everybody Loves Gina

Chapter 1

If you know anything about me, Angela Anaconda, you know I am stuck in a family with two unhuman ape older brothers, named Derek and Mark, who purposely ruin all my stuff, and a slobbery little baby sister named, Baby Lulu, who accidentally ruins all my stuff. So when I heard that Gina Lash, my best friend in the whole world, was actually coming to spend the whole entire weekend with us, you can imagine how excited and happy I was. Finally, someone on my side for once! Nobody has a best friend as good as Gina Lash.

"Hurry up and get here, Gina Lash, on account of I have some fun weekend plans planned for us," I said on the phone. "We can stay up all night, have pillow fights, make crank calls to Mrs Brinks…" This really was going to be the best weekend ever!

"Hello, is this Gina Lash, Angela's smarty pants friend? Who's smarter, you or your pants?" My big ape brother Mark yelled into the phone.

"You think your pants could do my homework while they're here?" My even bigger ape brother Derek added, like an idiot.

Then they tied me up with the phone cord and I started thinking that maybe having Gina Lash staying at our house wasn't such a good idea, after all. Gina Lash doesn't have any subhuman creatures at home to worry about. She lives alone with her mum, Liz Lash, who was going on a business trip to Acapulco that weekend, so that was why Gina Lash was staying with us. But before I knew it, a horn was honking in my driveway, which meant that my best friend was already here!

Mark and Derek had beaten me to the front door.

"You'd better leave Gina Lash alone this weekend," I told them.

"Oh, yeah? And what if we don't?" asked Mark.

Before I could think of a good answer, Gina Lash came up the driveway carrying a super special surprise sleepover pack! My two big animal brothers really wanted to get their grubby mitts on it, but I managed to shove Gina Lash out of their way.

"Come on, Gina Lash," I said. "Let's go and open your secret surprise sleepover pack in secret in my room with the door locked!"

"You won't make it to the door in a trillion years!" laughed Derek, as he and Mark started to chase after us.

Unhuman apes may be stronger and faster than human girls, but they are not smarter and they definitely do not have more brains than Gina Lash, smartest in the class. Instead of

7

trying to outrun them, which is what I wanted to do, Gina opened the box she was carrying and pulled out a tiny toy toaster.

"Here, you can play with this," she said.

Even I was surprised to see how interested those two big lame brains became in one little toy.

"Hey! A 'Cinch-y Bake Toaster'!" yelled Derek, as if it were a crate of waterproof firecrackers.

"Let's go and melt something! Yeah!" said Mark.

And they both disappeared in one second flat. Is Gina Lash a great best friend, or what?

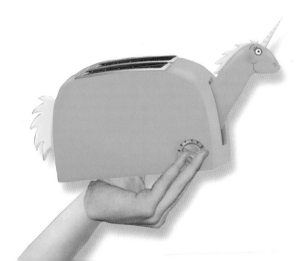

Chapter 2

So finally it was on to my room to really start the super fun activities for our super fun weekend sleepover!

"Mum just bought these pillows on clearance, cheap," I said to Gina Lash. We can beat each other senseless with them!"

Then, of course, that other pain in my neck, Baby Lulu, came in.

"Baby Lulu, no!" I said. "This is my room and there's no room for you in it!"

Instead of leaving like I asked her to, Baby Lulu started acting like a baby and crying at the top of her lungs. In order to calm her down, I sang her one of my little songs, which never fail to work.

"Hush little baby
Don't say a word.
Mama's gonna give you a big fat bird.

If that big fat bird won't fly,
Mama's gonna give you a kidney pie…"

But this time my song *did* fail to work and Baby Lulu just cried louder. *Now* what was I supposed to do?

"Hey," I wanted to yell. "I have very important company here!"

Then Gina Lash did something that I thought would never work. She picked up Baby Lulu. And just like that, Baby Lou stopped crying. Pretty great, right? But the only thing was, when I took Baby Lulu back, she started screaming at the top of her lungs again. She only liked Gina Lash. Okay, fine with me…I guess.

"Let's move on to the phone call part of our weekend!" I said.

There's nothing like making crank phone calls to your worst enemy (teacher's pet Nanette Manoir) with your best friend (Gina Lash). And off we went off to use the phone in the kitchen, where, too bad for us, those two bird-brained beasts, Derek and Mark, were playing paper football with a crumpled piece of paper at the kitchen table.

"AARGH, this is impossible!" cried Derek, as the paper fell off the table for the twentieth time.

"What's impossible?" asked Gina Lash.

I pulled Gina aside in order to stop her before it was too late.

"Stay away from them, Gina Lash! Just because you can make Baby Lulu stop crying doesn't mean you can make Mark and Derek stop being Mark and Derek. They'll end up eating you alive while you're still living!"

"We can't get the ball through the goals!" cried Mark, as if that was so important.

Instead of acting like my best friend and listening to me, Gina Lash actually took the time to refold the little paper football into a triangle.

"Your problem here is that you've got the wrong shape," she explained, talking to them as if they were real people! "Traditional desktop football is played with a triangular piece of paper, for aerodynamic reasons. There."

Then they tried the new and improved shape and, bingo, it worked!

"You rock, Gina Lash!" Derek yelled. And Mark was just

as happy.

Can you still be best friends with someone, if you don't share the same enemies? Some special sleepover weekend this was turning out to be. So far, no pillow fights, no crank phone calls and now my best friend was becoming friends with my enemy brothers who are not even human. Could it get worse? Oh yes it could. It seems *everybody* loved Gina Lash. Not just Mark, not just Derek and not just Baby Lulu.

Chapter 3

Before I knew it, Gina Lash was in my mum's art studio, posing as a model for a drawing mum was going to draw.

When I said it was time to make plans for our all night stay-up party, all she could answer was, "Angela, I'm kind of busy right now."

"Magnificent!" my mum was saying. "All the great models had big, beautiful curves. They're so much more fun to draw than knobbly knees…"

Have you ever seen my knees? Whenever my brothers call me toothpick peg legs, my mum, the same one who all of a sudden loved Gina Lash's big curves, always says, "I think your knobbly knees are sweet. One day, you'll grow into them."

Things seemed to be getting as bad as things could get. When I tried to get Gina to come and help me rig up a special dangerous revenge booby trap in my brothers' room, I found her out in the garden instead, with my dad. They were looking at his dead tomatoes. Can you think of anything more boring and unbestfriendly than that?

"Mr Anaconda, with a rake, a length of twine and a tablecloth, I think we could whip up enough shade to yield a bumper crop, just in time for ketchup-making season!" she was telling him.

I left them both in his workshop. Dad and Gina Lash were too busy designing a water system for the entire garden to even notice me leaving. If you had told me before this special sleepover weekend that I would be spending my special sleepover weekend complaining about my best friend Gina Lash, I would have told you that you were as crazy as Nanette Manoir's unFrench French. But that was what I was now doing with my other friends, Johnny Abatti and Gordy Rhinehart, complaining. The worst part was, they did not agree with me that this was such a big deal.

"It's not Gina Lash's fault that everyone loves her!" said

Gordy Rhinehart, like he was in love with Gina Lash himself, which everybody knows he is.

All Johnny Abatti could say was, "Hey! Angela's jealous that her family likes Gina Lash better than her!"

"I am not jealous. I'm glad that my family loves Gina Lash!" I said.

I know Johnny Abatti doesn't mean it, and that is just the way he is, but he can really say the wrong thing sometimes, that is, most of the time!

"Besides," I said to Gordy. "It's only for the weekend, right?"

So much for second best friends when it comes to problems with your first best friend.

17

Chapter 4

At dinner that night, everyone was excited to give me the bad news.

"Isn't it great, Angela?" my mother chirped like a happy bird. "Gina will be with us for two more weeks! Her mum had more business to take care of in Acapulco."

Mark and Derek were cheering. My dad was busy asking Gina Lash's advice about his asparagus plants.

"I've heard that chickens are good for that," said Gina Lash, the know-it-all expert. "They peck around the asparagus, eating the weeds, plus you get the benefit of free range eggs."

"Chickens! Cool!" said Derek, who hates every word that comes out of my mouth. Could Gina Lash say *anything* wrong?

And do you know what we happened to be having for dinner that night? None other than my most hated food, Tuna

Noodle Casserole.

"This is my favourite meal!" said Gina Lash.

Some best friend. We were having less and less in common the more she stayed at our house.

"Now that Gina's going to be here for another couple of weeks, we'll have to find something to entertain her with," said my mum. "Any ideas?"

Then, guess what, big surprise. Gina Lash know-it-all had another big idea. And if you ask me, it was a horrible one.

(But of course, no one asked me.)

"Well, once I read about a family that put on a carnival in their own backyard," said Gina.

What did she say? First she tells my dad to get chickens and he does. Then she comes up with this carnival idea and they all get too happy.

"Art booths!"

"Games!"

"Food!

"Oh, Gina Lash, what a wonderful idea!"

Chapter 5

And by the next weekend, we not only had a bunch of noisy chickens running around, we had a dunking tank, a candy floss machine, my mum dressed as a fortune-teller, a barbecue grill going, and the entire neighbourhood in our yard. It seemed like the whole world was having a great time at Gina Lash's idea of a carnival except for me. I was sitting in my room, looking out of the window at Gina Lash eating candy floss and

laughing with everyone. And I mean everyone.

"Not only have you hogged my entire family, you've hogged my entire *street*!" I was thinking. "None of this should've happened, Gina Lash! You're supposed to be my best friend…"

Then I thought, "How about we start this whole visit all over again, only this time we will do things *my* way!"

And I imagined Gina Lash just arriving with her suitcase. She is waving at me and smiling and I am waving with one hand and hiding something behind my back with the other. POW!

"Why would you want to be with my family, Gina Lash, when you can have a pillow fight with me?"

POW! Gina Lash doesn't have a pillow, but I sure do. POW! POW!

"What's the matter, Gina Lash, are you chicken?"

Then I break the pillow over her head and she is covered in feathers. And before my very eyes, Gina Lash, covered in feathers, has turned into a giant chicken, running around and

23

clucking through the garden. A very nice nature scene. And you know how my mum loves to paint nature scenes! Even Miss Know-it-all Chicken Lash is not prepared for what happens next as a giant paintbrush, dripping with paint, starts chasing her round.

Okay, Chicken Lash, let's hear it. "Help me! Help me!" Come on, say it. Aha, the paintbrush finally gets you and covers you in red paint. You look down at yourself and are ready to squawk.

"Cool," you say. "I'm like a living work of art."

What did you say? You're not supposed to act like this! You're supposed to say, "Help me! Help me!" Okay, maybe you aren't saying it now, but you will be saying it. Especially when Mark and Derek give you a lesson in aerodynamics. Then I see Chicken Lash transformed into a football. She gets kicked from one nitwit brother to the other. And she is still happy. And she is still having fun!

"Being kicked is not supposed to be fun!" I yell.

"But it is!" says the Football Lash, as she turns back into Gina Lash.

And then I was not imagining things any more. It was

really her and she was really standing there in my room. Hey, who did she think she was, putting her hand on my shoulder? "Face it, Angela, I know you're mad at me, but I'm your best friend," she said. "You can't stay mad at me no matter how hard you try."

"I can so, stay mad at you," I said. "You family-hogger who hogs families!"

But who was I kidding? I never should have been jealous of Gina Lash in the first place.

"You're right," I sighed, with my head still against the window. "I can't stay mad at you."

"So how come you aren't at the carnival with my whole family?"

Gina shrugged and sat down on my bed.

"Well, to be honest, the only reason I suggested the carnival was to keep them busy so I could spend some quality time with *you*. I don't know if you've noticed, but they haven't given me a moment's peace since I got here."

"So you came in here because you wanted to hang out with me and not them?" I asked.

"Well, that and the candy floss machine ran out of sugar," she said.

Good old Gina Lash! My best friend.

"Hey!" I said. "Let's finally open up that special surprise sleepover pack you brought!"

Then before we knew it, we were making crank phone calls to Nanette Manoir.

"Nanette, dear," I said into the phone. "This is Mrs Brinks!"

We did not expect Nanette Manoir to know who we really *were*, but the best thing was, that she did not know who we were *not*.

"You know I'd prefer it

26

if you didn't call me during my exfoliating time, Mrs Brinks," she said in a huff.

Just when we were about to give Nitzy Ditz a very special homework assignment, we had to stop because were laughing so hard. *Nobody* has a best friend as good as Gina Lash! I guess that's why everybody loves her.

Labour Pains

Chapter 1

One rotten day, when I, Angela Anaconda had to ride home from school with my even more rotten older brothers, I found out something that almost made me throw up even more than their terrible driving. On a pit stop to the Budgie Burger, which was the only good part of that ride home, I discovered that Derek and Mark, two of the most useless non-human brothers on the face of the earth, each get five dollars a week allowance. *Each!*

Since I don't get anything nearly as much, I decided to talk this over with my parents. Maybe some sort of mistake had been made and they didn't realize that I was being underpaid (or, as I think of it, cheated).

"My allowance is only a dollar twenty-five. How can Mark and Derek each get a weekly allowance of five dollars a week?" I asked them.

"Your brothers do twice as much around the house, honey," my mum said, as if that were a good reason.

"And they're twice as old as you," my dad said, which I *know* is not a good reason.

Walking to school the next day, none of my friends could believe how low my allowance was. When I asked them how much they got, I got mad all over again.

"I earn a well-deserved five," said Gina Lash (who is the smartest in the class, so maybe she *does* deserve a little more than the rest of us, but only a little). "But I believe the going rate is at least two-fifty, overtime notwithstanding," she added.

"Yeah," said Johnny Abatti. "I get two-fifty or two slices of pizza."

"I get three dollars a week," said Gordy. "Although I'm just as happy to get paid in trinkets and baubles."

I could not believe my ears!

"So everybody's allowance is higher than mine? It's not fair," I said. And I meant it.

"Especially considering all the work you do," said Gina Lash.

"Work?" I said. If anyone knows me at all, they know that I am too busy to do boring things like work, especially boring work around the house.

"You *do* do chores and stuff, don't you?" asked Gina Lash.

"Well," I said, trying to think of some chore I did. "I might take out the garbage once a week…"

"Therein lies the problem *and* the solution, Angela," said Gina Lash. "If you do extra chores around the house, your parents will have to pay you more."

Is Gina Lash smart or what? All I had to do was more work (or in my case, *some* work) to get more money! I may never be twice as old as my brothers, but I bet I could do twice as much work!

Chapter 2

It didn't take me long to put my plan into action. The next day was really hot and I helped my dad mow the lawn. Then I washed the car and gave Baby Lulu a bath with the hose at the same time.

Knowing that I was going to make all that money made it easy to do even *more* boring work. I cooked dinner for everyone and when my dad told my two dork-faced brothers to clean up the kitchen, I said they could go and watch their stupid "Rock-n-Wrestle Brain Smack" wrestling show on TV, and *I* cleaned up instead. I even hung the laundry on the line and did all these boring chores for an entire boring week, because I knew I was going to get paid a very unboring, real allowance for once.

When the end of the week rolled around and my mum said,
"You've been quite the helper around the house all week,
honey."

And my dad said, "We think you deserve a little extra." I
just knew I was in for at least five smack-a-roonies. At least!

"Here's your allowance," said my dad.

"And an extra fifty cents," said my mum.

What did they say? And in my hand they dropped my same old one dollar twenty-five allowance with fifty more measly cents! Did you ever work really, really super extra hard on really, really super extra boring things because you knew you were going to get a really big super extra reward when it was all over and not get it? At all?

"Fifty cents?!" I said. "But I did all that extra work!"

"Gosh, Angel-fish," said my Dad. "We thought you were just being nice because it was your mother's birthday last week."

"But a one-time bonus only once is not enough," I said (and I meant it too, especially a one-time bonus of a measly fifty cents!) "Gina Lash gets five dollars a week!"

"I know it may not seem fair to you," said my dad in that serious I-am-not-going- to-change-my-mind way that parents have. "But we feel we're paying you a reasonable amount for your age."

"Besides," said my mum, "Gina Lash is an only child."

"Great," I thought, as I was left there with my crummy allowance plus only fifty cents more after I did all that boring work all week. "Now I'm being punished on account of Mark and Derek being born. As if them being born isn't punishment enough."

I went off to Gina Lash's house to tell her how stupid her smart idea about me doing twice the work was. But, as usual, Gina Lash had an answer for everything. A smart answer.

"You really should have negotiated with your parents ahead of time," she said, after I told her the whole story.

"Negotiated?" I asked. Sometimes even *I* have trouble understanding what Gina Lash is talking about.

"You've got so much to learn about labour relations," sighed Gina Lash.

Whatever *that* means. Then, as she ate another pastry, she told me what it meant.

"Your situation isn't just about age discrimination, Angela," she said. "It's about the exploitation of the under-class. It's about fighting for what's right!"

Wow. Is Gina Lash smart or what?

"Besides, if we allow your parents to underpay you, it'll set a bad example for parents throughout Tapwater Springs."

"Yeah!" I said. *Everything* Gina Lash said made total sense.

"It's time for you to strike, Angela Anaconda!"

Strike? Like you see on TV? With picket signs and angry crowds and people throwing eggs and booing their cheap bosses? Okay!

"Sounds like a plan that is a plan to me, Gina Lash!"

The next day we were ready for action! Or in my case I was ready to do no actions, which is what you do when you go on strike. You do not do your job any more. And if you are like me and my friends, Johnny Abatti, Gordy Rhinehart and good old Gina Lash herself, you make signs to carry saying things like "Low Pay! No Way!".

We even started chanting, "Low Pay! No Way!" Just like real life strikers on TV!

"Why are we doing this again?" asked Johnny Abatti.

"Who cares," said Gordy in a very low voice. "I get to follow Gina Lash all day." (Everyone knows how madly in love with Gina Lash Gordy Rhinehart is.)

"Let's imagine that Mr and Mrs Anaconda are the dictatorial bosses of a multi-national corporation and Angela is their

underpaid employee," said Gina Lash, as if Johnny could ever understand a word she says. "Going on strike is the most effective way to protest and demand a higher wage."

Johnny thought about that important and interesting information for a minute and then said, "So why are we doing this again?"

And then those two dictatorial bosses themselves, my mum and dad, pulled up in the car and started unloading groceries.

"Hi, kids, what's going on?" asked my dad.

"Normally I would be helping you unload the groceries, Mum and Dad," I said. "But today I cannot on account of I am striking."

They didn't seem to understand a word I was saying. That is, until my best friend, Gina Lash, stepped in for me.

"With all due respect, Mr and Mrs Anaconda," she said. "We're supporting Angela's stance that her current allowance is unconscionably low."

Now, if you heard a very smart explanation like that, wouldn't you give me a rise in my allowance? I know *I* would. But my dad and mum would not.

"We've explained our position, Angela," said my mum.

"And we feel it's fair. But I guess you have a right to protest."

"Besides," said Dad, "it looks like you kids are having fun!"

The only fun we were having in that boring hot sun was watching them lug into the house all the groceries, which we were not helping them with. But then my mum had to stop and hold something up that almost ruined our strike.

"Oh – and we picked up some doughnuts from Mapperson's," she said. "I'll leave them on the table in case you rabble-rousers want a snack break."

As you know, Gina Lash is my best friend and has the smartest ideas. One of them was this strike against my family. But she does have things she loves besides smart ideas and one of them is Mapperson's Bakery and the doughnuts they bake. I could see Gina was very tempted to get off the picket line to go and get one.

"Don't give in, Gina Lash!" I said.

And because she is such a good friend, she didn't. But I knew how hard this was for

her. To tell you the truth, this strike was starting to get a little bit hard for all of us.

"This strike doesn't seem to be working very well, Gina Lash," I said. "On account of we're still striking."

"Just be patient, Angela Anaconda," said Gina Lash. "Even small-scale revolutions take time. The key to our strike is blocking anyone from doing any chores in your house."

But just as she said that, we heard the lawnmower rev up. My two dimwit brothers were about to cut the lawn!

"Hey!" I yelled. "You're crossing the picket line!"

"Too bad," said Mark. "We can't play Brain Smack on tall grass."

So much for stopping *them*. How was I supposed to strike from doing my chores, if my overpaid brothers did my chores for free? Gina Lash saw how upset I was getting.

"Don't worry, Angela. We'll strike until justice is served!" she said.

Then she sniffed the air. Was that food? Oh no, it *was* getting past lunchtime.

"Or until lunch is served," said Gina Lash. "Gotta go!"

Chapter 4

Okay, so Gina Lash left us to go and eat lunch. She would be back. That's what I kept telling Gordy Rhinehart and Johnny Abatti. At least they were still picketing with me. That is, until my dad came out of the garage, dropping pieces of wood he was carrying.

"Need any help, Mr Anaconda?" asked Gordy.

And before you could say, "Low Pay! No Way!", Gordy was helping my dad carry everything away.

"Gordy, what are you doing?" I asked.

"He's an old man," said Gordy. "His back could snap."

So much for solidarity. No Gina Lash. No Gordy Rhinehart. Just me and Johnny Abatti.

"I guess you really learn who your friends are," I said to Johnny.

"Yeah, well," yawned Johnny Abatti. "I promised Nonna I'd help out at the pizza parlour. See ya!"

There I was, the only one on strike and the strike wasn't even over yet. It seemed like I had spent another twenty hours in the hot sun, picketing my house, not giving in, waiting for at least Gina Lash to get back and join me, when I got really thirsty. As I went over to get a drink of water out of the garden hose, I saw something that was worse than I could ever imagine. In the kitchen, at the table, eating doughnuts with my parents who would not give me a bigger allowance, was none other than my best friend in all the world, Gina Lash!

"Well, from now on," I thought, "the only striking I will do is striking it rich!"

All I could imagine was sticking my picket sign into the ground and striking oil. Then I would be the boss and

everyone would work for me! That includes Derek and Mark
who, dressed as chauffeurs, will have to drive me everywhere
I want to go. Only they would drive carefully and well. And
as they take me home to my mansion, they will roll out a red
carpet for me.

"And since you crossed my picket line," I will tell them, "I am
sure you will not mind painting my picket fence."

I will yank on the red carpet, sending them flying into the air,

where they will land next to the longest picket fence in the world. As they are busy endlessly painting that endlessly long picket fence, I will whistle for my other workers, who are none other than my faithless friends who had struck out on my strike.

"Here are some water buckets full of soapy water," I will tell them. " As I wash my hands of you, you must wash everything and everybody."

After I watch them wash my giant car, my giant house, my beautiful big furniture, my dork-faced brothers and Baby Lulu and hang everything on a clothesline, justice will be served. Then dinner will be served.

"Bring me some fast food and make it fast!" I will demand. All this hard work has sure made me hungry!

After I eat my delicious favourite food, I will throw the dishes over my shoulder for my workers to catch and clean up after.

"Congratulations, my chore-loving chumps!" I will say. "You have finally earned your earnings. I suppose I will allow you your allowance! It won't cost me but a pretty penny."

Then Mark, Derek, Gordy Rhinehart, Johnny Abatti and

especially Gina Lash will line up, as I toss one measly penny each
into their beggars' cups.

"Don't spend it all in one place!" I say as the clink, clink *sound*
of the money hitting the cups gets awfully loud and real.

And there, leaving the front door of my house was that
doughnut-eating traitor, Gina Lash! To add insult to injury, she
was even getting some change from my parents. A lot of
change! My dimwit brothers, who were playing football on the
newly cut lawn, laughed at me.

"Looks like Gina Lash is an even bigger scab than we are!"
they said.

And this made me even madder.

"How could you go against me, Gina Lash?" I asked.

"How could I indeed, Angela Anaconda," she said. "When
I've just spent the last two hours conducting intensive labour
negotiations on your behalf?"

"You have?' I asked. "What does that mean?"

"It means I've got you a rise," said Gina Lash, as she
handed me a pile of extra money.

A permanent rise in my allowance? How could I have ever doubted my best and smartest friend, Gina Lash?

"You will have to take out the garbage three times a week," she said. "Like they say, Angela, there's no such thing as a free lunch!"

"Well there is today, Gina Lash," I said. "Come on, lunch is on me!"

Nobody has a friend as good as Gina Lash!

100 Yard Lash

Chapter 1

When you hear the name Gina Lash, what do you think of? Smartest in the class? Tiny Dottie Cakes? Cinnamon Swirls from Mapperson's Bakery? The love of Gordy Rhinehart's life? My very best friend? You're right about *all* of those things. But now I am going to tell you about a side to Gina Lash that you never knew existed. The superstar athlete side!

It was the day of the big kick-off and we were choosing this year's team captains for our annual school relay race. Coach Rhinehart picked me, Angela Anaconda, to be the captain of

Team Lemons on account of the fact that I nearly knocked Johnny Abatti's head off with the soccer ball. Then Mrs Brinks picked Miss Do-Nothing Teacher's Pet herself, Ninnie Wart Manoir (also known as Nanette), to be captain of the Limes.

But nothing could ruin my day, on account of the best part about winning the relay race is the top-secret prize that goes to the winning team. Even Coach Rhinehart did not know what the top-secret prize was. As he was opening the top-secret envelope to take a look, I told Johnny Abatti to climb up in the jungle gym behind him to see if he could see what was written on the paper inside the envelope. Since I am the team captain and everyone should listen to me, Johnny climbed up, even though he was

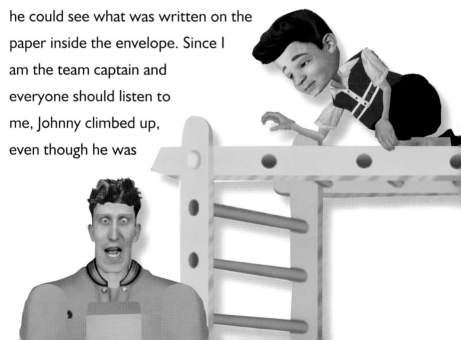

still dizzy from being hit in the head with the soccer ball.

This year's special secret prize seemed especially special by the look on Coach Rhinehart's face. Too bad Johnny Abatti bent over too far and fell on his head. At least he got a little bit of a peek at the secret prize first though.

"M.B., M.B.," he kept muttering, like someone who's fallen on his head one too many times. "All I could see was M.B…"

"As in melon ball?" I asked. Leave it to Johnny to only get the *initials* of the secret prize and not a complete word.

"Marcel's Boutique!" yelled Nanette Manoir. "That *must* be this year's top secret prize!"

Gina Lash, smartest in the class, is usually very busy reading books and eating doughnuts during gym class, but the mystery of the secret prize initials even got her interested.

"I seriously doubt it," she said, looking up from her book. "All the other secret prize winners got victory meals."

"Yeah," I said. "Last year's winners got 'All-You-Can-Eat' at the 'B.B.', meaning the Budgie Burger."

"So," said Gina Lash, as if she was a detective (which she is smart enough to be), "M.B. must stand for some purveyor of fine foods."

Gina Lash had a point, but all this guessing about the secret prize would have to wait. It was now time for the team captains to choose sides!

"Don't look at me, Angela Anaconda," said Gina Lash.

"I wouldn't think of it, Gina Lash," I told her. And that was true. Gina Lash was not known as the athletic type.

Too bad for Ninnie-Poo, Lemons got first pick and Limes did not and I picked Johnny Abatti.

"It's not fair!" whined Nanette. "I was going to pick Johnny Abatti! Okay then, I get two picks…"

So she picked the clone drones, January and Karlene. And even though Gordy Rhinehart is not so fast, I picked him because his dad had picked me for captain.

"Final cut!" yelled Coach Rhinehart. "Captains, choose your last legs!"

I was about to pick Jimmy Jamal, who is a really good runner even though he is always paying more attention to his video game, when something strange happened. Gina Lash was jumping up and down and waving to me.

"Angela! Angela! Pick me!" she was yelling.

What did she say? Gina Lash does not like to run. Then I saw the napkin from her doughnut in her hand. Mapperson's Bakery – M.B. The top-secret prize was probably "All-You-Can-Eat" at Mapperson's Bakery!

"Don't pick her," said Johnny Abatti. "Pick Jimmy. He's got Air Robosoles – they 'eat the road and spit out the competition'."

"I know that, Johnny Abatti, but Gina Lash *is* my best friend," I said.

"Pick ME, Angela Anaconda. I'm your man!" said Gina Lash.

"Don't pick her," said Johnny. "She's the slowest in the whole school!"

I have to admit, at least this once, Johnny was right about that. *Anyone* can run faster than Gina Lash.

"Hurry up, Angela Anaconda," said the horrible voice of my enemy, the baloney-headed captain of Team Limes. "Some of us have better things to do than sit around and wait for you to betray your best friend."

That did it! "Gina Lash," I said.

Even though it made Johnny smack himself in his sore head when Nanette got Jimmy Jamal for Team Limes, and

made me realize that we would have a hard time winning, it made Gina Lash happy. Very happy.

"Mapperson's Bakery!" she yelled, as if we had already won and were about to go and eat the top-secret prize.

"See you at the races, Angela," laughed Miss Nit. "Don't forget to bring the lemon-*aid*, since you'll need all the *aid* you can get!"

To tell you the truth, even though she is a do-nothing teacher's pet, even Nanette and her clone drones could run faster than Gina Lash, who has a pet turtle, Sheldon, and runs even less fast than he does. With Jimmy Jamal and his Air Robosoles on Team Limes, I had to come up with a top-secret plan if Team Lemons (my team) was going to win that top-secret prize.

Chapter 2

The next morning we started our heavy-duty training. Our first challenge was to get Gina Lash to run round the block.

"I can't run on an empty stomach," said Gina.

"Just think about how *un*-empty your stomach will be when we win all-you-can-eat at Mapperson's," I said, using some trick psychology, which is what all team captains should use. "Now you run round the block, and I'll wait here and time you."

But I was not the only one using trick psychology.

"One Mississippi, two Mississippi..." I was counting. Gina Lash left my sight at 239 Mississippi, slow but steady. When I reached 1,203 Mississippi, she came back into view. Not bad! It took her only about twenty times longer than Johnny Abatti and ten times longer than Gordy. Hey, Team Lemons has a real shot here, I thought.

"Great, Gina Lash!" I said. "You made it round the

block and you're not even sweating!"

As soon as I said that, the Manoir's Town Car pulled up and the Nanasty one threw a little aluminium foil swan at us. Like the kind you get in a restaurant when you don't finish all of your food.

"Oh, Gina," she said. "You left your doggie bag in the backseat. *Au revoir*, Angela Anaconda. We'll save you a place at the finish line!"

Gina Lash had not been running round the block. At all. She had not even been walking. She had been sitting in the backseat of Nanette Manoir's car, eating!

That did it! Secret plans call for secret weapons. We had to get serious here and that meant Gordy Rhinehart. We would use his undying love for Gina Lash to save us from our undying chances to lose.

"Until we race, Gordy will never leave your side, Gina Lash," I said.

"Never ever?" asked Gina Lash, as if this could not be true.

"Keep your eyes on the prize, remember? Mapperson's Bakery..." is all I said back.

And you know what? It worked! With Gordy's devoted,

love-sick help, Gina Lash went from being a person who did absolutely *no* exercise ever to someone who did a *little* bit of exercise when she was forced to. And since Johnny and I are great runners and Gordy Rhinehart is an okay runner, that is all we needed to win against Ninnie Wart and her gang, who were bad (Nanette) to okay (January and Karlene) runners but who had one great runner (Jimmy Jamal).

So finally the day of the big race arrived at last and there was the not so fast captain of Team Limes going through a trunk of designer green uniforms looking for the right one to wear, when she saw the new improved Gina Lash jog (not walk huffing and puffing) by.

"Excuse me, *please*. But do any of us really believe that Gina Lash could be that buff after only a few days of training? She should be tested for steroids!" she cried.

"Yeah," I said. "Like you should be tested for haemorrhoids, Nanette. Besides, Gina Lash is way too smart to be that stupid."

And before we knew it, it was line-up time! I was first runner on our team and Jimmy Jamal was first for Team Limes. And we were off! Good thing for Team Lemons, Jimmy Jamal never put down that video game and his batteries ran out in the middle of one of his highest scores. Because Johnny was right, those Robosoles really do eat up the road and if I am a great runner, Jimmy Jamal is a greater one, but because of his stopping to check his dead batteries, I was able to zoom ahead and hand the baton over to Johnny Abatti. And all while Ninky-Wink was still looking in her trunk for something to wear.

By the time Johnny had handed the baton over to Gordy, we had a nice, big lead. And after Gordy, it was Gina Lash's turn to tear up the track. Like I say, we had Gina Lash in good enough shape to keep moving to the finish line. I didn't say, *race* to the finish.

Too bad for Ninky Wink, she had to run in a most unsuitable outfit. She finally stopped going through her trunk, when Gina Lash was half way to the finish line. Then she started running as fast as she could, and she still could not catch up with Gina Lash (who, remember, runs less fast than her pet turtle, Sheldon). Then, too bad for us, Ninky-Wink tried a most unsuitable trick by grabbing the back of Gina Lash's elastic Lemon-coloured pinny. But instead of pulling Gina Lash back with the Team Lime losers, the elastic broke and Gina Lash shot over the finish line like the winning Lemon she is.

"The best thing about winning is that Team Lemons beat Limes and we're getting the top-secret prize," I said, as Johnny and Gordy jumped round Gina Lash, who had no more energy and was lying flat on the ground. "But the second best thing is that we never have to do *that* again, especially Gina Lash!"

But just as Coach Rhinehart was going to raise my triumphant captain's arm in triumph, we heard the screech of that losing Lime, teacher's pet.

"Mrs Brinks! Mrs Brinks!" shrieked Nanette. "I hadn't decided on my outfit. I had to run with the sun in my eyes! Gina Lash took up two lanes, my

beauty queen mother never encouraged me to take an interest in athletics…"

"Oh, you poor dear," said Mrs Brinks, who only likes Nanette and no one else. "You are so right. Do over!"

"Do what?" asked Johnny Abatti.

By the time we got Gina Lash up in a standing position, we looked up just in time to see Team Lime crossing the finishing line. And there we were, the losing team who never even got to the starting line!

Chapter 4

There was only one thing worse than not getting the top-secret prize and that was having to sit there and watch the green queen of mean make a speech at the awards ceremony.

"Though I carried us to victory, it was truly a team effort…" she was saying and we were all about to throw up from listening to her, and I was getting very mad on account of the fact that the cheaters always seem to win.

"We'll show you 'team effort' Ninnie-not-so-fast Manoir," I was thinking, as I saw my Team Lemons lining up on the track and me lassoing Nanette with the finishing line tape.

"Have no fear, baloney-head. We superior Lemons will be delighted to carry you to victory…" I say, as she bounces like a pinball from one Lemon team member to the other.

"Help me, help me! Oh great Captain Angela," I can hear you say. "Better Captain than I, whom I wish I could do over my entire

relationship with," you will tell me as I trip you with the baton, instead of passing it to you. But don't fret, Gina Lash has baked you a triple crème pie to soften your fall. Since you need to bulk up, and you know how Gina likes to add steroids to everything, we will watch you turn from Thin Nin into a Giant Nincompoop. We do hope that Marcel's Boutique carries something bigger than petite. Because you are bigger than any giant we've ever seen, Neander Nanette. And you have a nice big shiny trophy to prove it.

"But excuse me, please, obnoxious Nin," I say into a megaphone because you are so high in the sky. "I believe that trophy belongs to us!"

I climb up on the backs of my winning Team Lemons as they form a human pyramid and I am able to pluck the winning trophy out of your losing hands and AAAHH...

My folding chair collapsed just as Coach Rhinehart got up to award the top-secret grand prize.

"I'll give you a little hint," he said, trying to keep the suspense. "The initials are M.B."

"I just know it's Marcel's Boutique..." Nin the Pinny-Puller was saying to her clone drone club, January and Karlene. Jimmy Jamal was busy winning another game on his game player. He couldn't care less.

"This year's grand prize," said Coach Rhinehart, still dragging out the suspense, "is a home-cooked liver loaf and boiled potatoes supper at the home of our own Mrs Brinks!"

And he said Mrs Brinks concentrating on the "M" in Mrs and the "B" in Brinks. Were we lucky to lose, or what?

"And she's throwing in an all-you-can-watch slideshow of her recent road trip with Mr Brinks to the Lake Winnewanka Ice Fishing Jubilee!" he added.

The only thing better than losing that top-secret first prize was watching how angry Not-So-Fast Nanette was.

"*Slide show?*" she shrieked. "I've been robbed!"

And just when I thought things could not get any better, they did.

"And for the hard working runners-up, all-you-can-eat desserts at Mapperson's Bakery!" concluded Coach Rhinehart.

"Come on, Gina Lash!" I said. "We've got some serious carbo-loading to do!"

This was a great day for Team Lemons. We all tried to pick up Gina Lash and carry her to Mapperson's, but we almost got crushed to death, so we ended up putting her down.

"First one there's a rotten egg!" said Gina Lash, because she is the smartest in the class and knew this was a good way to keep us all from running there. She did want to get there as soon as possible. It's just that one race is enough in one day.

We left Ninny behind in the distance, holding up her top-secret grand prize and crying, "It's not fair! Do over! Do over!"

MAPPERSON'S DAUGHTER

CHAPTER 1

One day, in art class, Gordy Rhinehart got me, Angela Anaconda, and my friends Johnny Abatti and Gina Lash to make a papier mâché giraffe out of newspapers for our group art project. Even though Gordy was the only one who really cared about it, I have to admit that this giraffe was turning out pretty well.

"I think we should name him Bennie," said Gordy. "A name with a quiet dignity, so typical of his species."

Gina Lash was passing the newspaper pieces to Johnny and Gordy to make our giraffe, when she found a ripped-in-half article about her favourite place on earth. "Mapperson's!" she said.

The other half of the article had already become part of Bennie's body, but that didn't stop Gina Lash, who started to unravel him in no time flat. That's how important news about Mapperson's Bakery is to her!

"It's all smudgy," said Gina, trying to piece together the article. *"Retired?"* she yelled. Then she ran out of art class, just like that!

I have to admit that, even though Gordy was upset about having to bandage up Bennie, this was becoming a very exciting day. We followed Gina Lash to Mapperson's Bakery.

"Don't do it, Mr Mapperson! Don't retire!" Gina Lash was yelling. "If I don't get my daily dose of Cinnamon Swirls, I'll lose my mind!"

Mr Mapperson just smiled and patted Gina on the head.

"Don't worry, Gina," he said. "I'm not retiring. The bakery truck is."

And we all looked at the old Mapperson's Bakery truck. It was so old that the boy in the picture on the truck probably went to grade school with Mrs Brinks, our teacher, who is not young at all.

"As soon as I pick a new face for the new truck, we'll be back on the road," said Mr Mapperson. "Say, I don't suppose any of you kids would want your face on a truck?"

Who wouldn't want to be the Mapperson's truck face? Then Mr Mapperson told us to each bring in a picture tomorrow, and he would pick his favourite to be the face on the side of his new bakery truck!

"You hear that?" said Johnny Abatti. "One of us gets to be the new Mapperson's truck face!"

"Whatever you do, don't tell anybody anything," I said. This way, I figured, Mr Mapperson would be sure to choose *one* of our faces (hopefully, *my* face) to be the face on the side of the truck.

The next day had a few more surprises for us. Johnny, Gordy and I all went back to Mapperson's with our best pictures of ourselves. We knew, of course, that Gina Lash would be there before us. She is there first thing every day for her favourite Mapperson creation, Cinnamon Swirls. And we were right. Gina Lash was there. But she had no picture.

"Where's *your* picture, Gina Lash?"

"I'm not entering," she said. "People should buy Mapperson's pasteries because they're a quality

77

product. Not because they've been dazzled by my good looks on the side of a truck. Besides, I have issues with the exploitation of my image for commercial gain."

Whatever *that* means. To tell you the truth, I was glad. Now I had an even better chance to see my face on the side of its very own truck. But then the second surprise of the day happened. Before you could say "Cinnamon Swirls", every kid in town arrived at the bakery, waving a picture of themselves.

"I don't get it," I said. "How did everyone find out?"

Johnny Abatti shrugged. "Er…I may have told a few people at the pizza parlour last night," he said.

Now I know he doesn't mean it and that is just the way he is, but Johnny Abatti does some things that are not very smart, probably because Johnny is not very smart. Okay, so there are now like one million kids in Mapperson's Bakery, all waving pictures of themselves at Mr Mapperson, all wanting to be on the side of the truck. What could be worse, you say?

"Mr Mapperson! Mr Mapperson! I hope it's not too late for me, officially the prettiest girl in Tapwater Springs, to submit a professionally photographed entry portrait." You are right! Nanette Manoir, Miss Teacher's Pet herself, who ordinarily would not be caught dead at Mapperson's Bakery because they do not serve fancy French pastries full of cream which make you throw up, was waving not one picture of herself, but an entire fashion model's portfolio. In other words, at least ten pictures of herself! And the worse thing was that Mr Mapperson thought they were nice!

"Wow!" he said. "Very impressive, Nanette."

Chapter 3

In school later that day, no one was busy trading lunches or having secret food fights in the cafeteria. We were all excited about the Mapperson Truck Contest, but not in a good way. More like in the way you get when you have to take an important test which you know you do not know the answers to. The first to crack under all this pressure was Gordy.

"Um, Gordy, you gonna eat that doughnut?" Gina Lash asked him at our lunch table.

Instead of blushing and giving Gina Lash anything she asks for, which is what Gordy usually does because he is in love with her, Gordy jumped up and started screaming, "That's it! Enough about Mapperson's Bakery! I can't take it any more! Bennie and I are withdrawing our picture!"

Gina was a little shocked at Gordy's behaviour, but hey, he *did* leave her the doughnut.

"Another face bites the dust," is what I thought.

And really, what had looked like an impossible contest to win, started to get easier.

Chapter 4

That afternoon, when Johnny Abatti and I walked Gina Lash to Mapperson's for her daily afternoon treat, we saw Josephine Praline running out of the bakery screaming,

"A burnt muffin! It's a sign! I should never have entered a contest fraught with such vanities!"

Inside the bakery, Mr Mapperson was throwing out a tray of burnt muffins.

"Mr Mapperson," said Gina Lash sternly. "This contest is taking you away from your baking."

"Ah, don't worry, Gina," he said. "There's hardly any faces left in the running."

He told us that Candy May had dropped out because she thought that putting her face on the side of a truck would hurt. Jimmy Jamal had run into a tree and really had hurt his face, and then Johnny Abatti remembered that he couldn't be in it because Nonna said that if he used his beautiful face to endorse any products other than Abatti's Pizza, she would give him the evil eye.

"Fact is," said Mr Mapperson, "the only kids left in the contest are Angela and …"

"Hello, Gina Lash … and friends of Gina Lash."

Yup, you know who came in next. My baloney-headed arch-enemy and the only other face left in the contest besides my own.

"Hello, Nanette," said Mr Mapperson. "What brings you here?"

Little Miss Ninnie Wart snapped her fingers and in came her slave/servant Alfredo, wearing a sandwich board with a giant nightmare-sized portrait of her monstrous face on it.

"I've decided to give the town a little preview of my face, so they can get used to seeing me everywhere. *Et voila!*" Nanette exclaimed.

Even Gina Lash was not so in the mood for a delicious treat after seeing that picture of Nanette's big lug head, which poor Alfredo had to drag around and Johnny Abatti (because he is not very smart) could not wait to try on. Unfortunately, Mr Mapperson thought it was great.

"Very impressive," he said with a smile.

"Walk around the block until I say so!" Nanette yelled at Johnny Abatti and Alfredo. "Go! Go!"

Mr Mapperson smiled as he watched them leave. This was the second time he had said that something Pin Nin did was impressive, so I figured I had better come up with an impressive plan myself.

Chapter 5

And the next day I did. Thanks to my dad's Squeegee-Easy. Why not wash Mr Mapperson's Bakery window, I thought? Isn't *that* an impressive thing to do? And so, there I was, bright and early, before school, using the Squeegee-Easy to wash Mr Mapperson's window. It was sort of fun and I started to sing one of my songs:

> *"I'll wash his window and with some luck*
>
>   *He'll put my face up on the truck.*

Then that somebody will frown and fret

'Cause he picked me and not…"

"What a charming singing voice. I'm surprised every dog in town isn't howling along," said the voice of my most hated arch-enemy in the world.

"Nanette?" I asked. Even though I knew who it was, I was still surprised to see her, especially this early in the morning.

But before I could think up something to say, Nanette did something which *I* thought was good, but *she* thought was horrible. She stepped back into my bucket of dirty water and the Squeegee-Easy hit her square in the face. She was doused in the window-cleaning water. I sure do love that Squeegee-Easy!

"You won't get away with this, Angela Anaconda!" she was screaming.

But before she could finish, Mr Mapperson came along to open the bakery. He was really happy.

"Wow! Those windows never looked cleaner!" he said. "Nice job, Nanette!"

Nanette? *What* did he say? Then I realized that because Ninky Dink was all covered in water, Mr Mapperson thought that she was the one who had been hard at work. And then, of course,

Nanette had to tell him how she thought that the clean windows would make it easier for everyone to see his *wonderful* baked goods (as if she ever ate any of them).

And Mr Mapperson said, "That's the kind of considerate kid you want on a bakery truck."

Which made me almost crazy until Gina Lash (who you would *expect* to be at Mapperson's Bakery before it opened) came along and said, "Don't you get it, Angela? The only thing that matters about Mapperson's is the product."

Another good idea from Gina Lash, smartest in the class! I ran inside the bakery, and even though I had eaten breakfast at home, I ordered a muffin. Mr Mapperson was very happy to serve me until you-know-who appeared, speaking her phoney unFrench French.

"Only one, Angela Anaconda? They are so *très magnifique,* Mr Mapperson, that I'll have three!"

Before Mr Mapperson could say, "Very impressive, Nanette," I ordered a baker's dozen, which is not twelve muffins but thirteen! So *there*, Ninky Wink! But then Nanetter ordered another ten muffins too. Uh oh, I don't even think Gina Lash, Mr Mapperson's biggest fan, could eat thirteen muffins after breakfast at home. But somehow, Nanette could. We sat there eating muffins all morning, while Mr Mapperson just smiled. Then, just as I was about to *throw* up or *give* up, I'm not sure which, Mr Mapperson came over with a tray of steaming hot cookies.

"Care to sample my new Double-Chocolate, Macadamia Sugar, Sugar Snaps?" he asked.

I could not even say "no", my stomach was so full. But Miss Goody-Good-for-nothing ate one as easy as pie.

"I think it's quite rude to turn down food, especially when there are starving children in the world, don't you, Angela?" she asked. This made me even sicker and Mr Mapperson even happier.

"I like your attitude, Nanette," he said, as Ninnyworms got

up from the table, looking as if she had only eaten a little tiny sugar cookie and not thirteen muffins. Which is what I discovered had in fact really happened, when I looked down at the floor where she had been sitting and saw her not-so-perky little poodle, Oo-La-La, looking almost as sick and full as I was! So *that's* who had been eating all of Nanette's muffins!

"Maybe I could have my face on a truck if I cheated, too, Cheater-Cheater, Poodle-Feeder!" I thought to myself.

Then I thought, so what, let Nanette put her big unFrench face on the side of the bakery truck. What she doesn't know, is that I am driving another truck. Yes, little Nin, we are competing in the Bakery Truck Demolition Derby!

"Oh, don't scream like a Ninnie," I will say as I race my truck straight into you. Aha, you have swerved and I've covered you in mud! Don't worry, my dad's Squeegee-Easy will clean you in a jiffy!

"Help me! Help me! Oh Angela, whose face deserves to be on a truck more than mine!" You will scream. Oh

no, what's this? I have cleaned you off the truck and you have landed into a vat of dough!

"Maybe you just need to be kneaded," I say as I flatten you out, flat as a pancake. Maybe I will make truck cookies out of you, but, "Oh no, I'm sorry your face did not make the final cut," I will say, as I roll you back up and toss you back into the dough vat and bake you into muffins. But even Oo-la-Cheater, your little poodle, will not eat you, you leave such a bitter taste.

As I throw the muffin away, Mr Mapperson is annoyed.

"You're not only going to have to clean up this mess," he says. "But pay for it too."

I look at the pile of half-eaten muffins left by Oo-blah-da and want to just scream, but I can't, I am too full.

Chapter 6

The next day, when the new truck was to be unveiled at the bakery, I only went along because all the kids in town wanted to see whose picture was on it.

"Well, Angela," said someone who I do not even want to mention because I thought we would probably be seeing her big giant head on the side of a truck until we were all older than Mrs Brinks. "I hope you're not too disappointed by the results. After all, you were *très* out of your league!"

Then Mr Mapperson gave a little speech about how he had picked the perfect and most deserving kid in town to be the face on his truck, and as he pulled the sheet off the side of the truck, Nanette stepped up to take a bow. But then something really great that no one expected happened. Nanette looked at the side of the truck and started screaming as if she were in a horror movie.

"Gina Lash?" she shrieked, as if it was the end of the world.

And there on the side of the new Mapperson's Bakery truck was a smiling picture of my best friend, Gina Lash.

"But Mr Mapperson," said Gina, getting a little upset. "I didn't even give you my picture."

"I didn't need one," he said. "You're in the store every day. What other face would you choose to grace the truck, but the one belonging to my best customer!"

And before Gina Lash could say "no", which is what she was about to say, Mr Mapperson promised her all-you-can-eat Cinnamon Swirls.

"For the rest of my life?" asked Gina, all happy.

"No, for the rest of the day," he said.

"Good enough!" said Gina Lash. But then, because she is my best friend, Gina Lash turned to me. "No hard feelings, Angela Anaconda? I know you wanted to be on that truck. And you must be jealous of my all-you-can-eat Cinnamon Swirls."

I just shook my head. "Actually, Gina Lash, if I never see another Mapperson's treat again, I'll be just fine.

THE END

"Hi, if you've enjoyed this book, why not read some more books about me, Angela Anaconda, and the other folks at Tapwater Springs. We have a cool selection."

Coming Soon . . .

GORDY RHINEHART'S RAINY DAY ACTIVITY BOOK

NANETTE'S GUIDE TO BEING (BUTT-KISSING) PERFECT

PIZZA WARS